T

THE LITTLE BOOK

OF

JOHN B. KEANE

MERCIER PRESS

MERCIER PRESS
5 French Church Street, Cork
16 Hume Street, Dublin 2

Trade enquiries to CMD DISTRIBUTION,
55a Spruce Avenue, Stillorgan Industrial Park,
Blackrock, Dublin

© John B. Keane 2000

ISBN 1 85635 321 4
A CIP record for this book is available from the British Library.

10 9 8 7 6 5 4 3 2 1

TO DANNY AND EILEEN HANNON

Printed in Ireland by Colour Books Ltd.

Your theological rantings have the same effect on the people of Listowel as the droppings of an underfed blackbird on the water levels of the Grand Coulee Dam.

That same God ... gave man dominion over the fowl and the brute, over every corner of the land and sea but man has no dominion at all over his own flute and the tunes it's likely to play and that's a thing all men must remember when shame reddens the cheek.

The emphasised indifference of the true snob.

There's enough lies written on the headstones of Ireland without my adding to them.

That unique repository of monumental hyperbole, the common graveyard.

The propagation of bingo is the ultimate role of the Catholic Church in Ireland.

There was more honesty when I was a boy. I often saw three or four eating out of the same plate and they didn't wrong each other a crumb.

Thirty years in Dáil Éireann and never opened his mouth except to pick his teeth.

A creaking step is as good as a dog and it eats very little, just a fragment of wax polish now and then.

For the protection of the inmates, if nothing else, every household should have its own visiting hours.

There came a merciful silence during which the clock was given a chance to air its views.

To cure his arthritis he singed his bare bottom with burning newspapers as they once did to clear recalcitrant feathers from the carcasses of hastily-plucked geese.

He travelled widely and spoke numerous languages including Gaelic, Australian, Canadian and New Zealandese.

A play about sex in Ireland is always ahead of its time.

Be anything, a spy, an informer, even a pimp or a hangman but don't be an actor!

Obscurity is the best bodyguard.

Bravery was bravery no matter which side a man took in any conflict.

A county is an organisation that revels in its own imagined supremacy and then, to cover its inadequacies, makes cheap jokes at the expense of its more illustrious neighbours.

Ever mindful of his madcap rugby days he seized her by the Havelock Road end.

It was a sneeze that loosened a nose-ful of ancient and hitherto inextir-pable snots.

The most approachable benefactor of bladder and bowel, the public toilet.

He had been apprenticed for a while to a country pig-killer. On his mantel-piece was a long-denuded spare rib and a pickled snout to remind him of his inconsequent ancestry.

He was as fine a figure of a man as ever took leave of a woman's womb.

The achievement of a man who over-writes is as valueless as that of a losing horse which reserves its best efforts for when it passes the winning post.

It's enthusiasm, not enthusiism. Suppose they called one of your orgasms an orgism.

Truth is the most evasive of all commodities. It's too hot to handle and too prickly to hold. It simply won't let itself be told.

An affair is like an air-filled toy balloon which takes off madly in all directions when its wind is released. It rasps, wheezes, snorts, squeaks and screeches with a passion unbridled and then flops on the floor, a parody of its former self.

All boys have insatiable appetites especially after their dinners.

―――――❖―――――

Inside every bald-headed man is a natural hair repellent.

―――――❖―――――

When a man wrestles with his conscience all the weight is on his side.

―――――❖―――――

If that man was to stand on his merits ... he'd be the tallest man in the five parishes.

―――――❖―――――

'Thanks be to God we have our health,' said Dick Roche from his wheelchair.

When the curate broke wind for the third time my father turned to me and said, 'that, my boy, is liturgical farting at its finest.'

Don't worry ... your celibacy is in no danger. The tastes of these fine ladies run to the cockerel rather than the rooster.

Many a worshipful devotee will tell you that, of all the world's vistas, the female posterior is the most surpassing. Even the most chaste will not deny that in its unclad glory it is the most intoxicating of all prospects.

There's many a regal gander no more than skin and bones in his pelt.

Maybe England was the mother of parliaments but she was also the wicked stepmother of Ireland.

There are many Irish women like sports-cars with speeds of one hundred and fifty miles an hour but moving at only forty-five.

Impregnated by his hairy jokes she gave birth, after awhile, to a fine healthy yawn.

I don't mind a person having false teeth or false eyelashes. I'd be far more concerned about false pretenses.

Booze to the sober man is what flood-waters are to the stranded fish, what the starting pistol is to the straining athlete, what the sound of the whistle is to the waiting midfielder.

I'll serve my betters and I'll serve my equals but I won't be a housemaid to trash.

As the candle's flame deludes the moth so does the cultivated accent delude the fool.

If you're seeking the source of humming which is musically expressive and linguistically effective ask one of your relatives for the loan of a substantial sum of money.

What is he anyway but a pampered oul' dotard with his roast and boiled every day and half the world starving.

A magpie has no more to do with bad luck than a meat pie.

Those hairs thou hast and their adoption tried, grapple them to thy poll with hoops of steel.

There wasn't as much lean in the bacon as you'd draw with a single stroke of a red biro.

Of course I knew Rodgers and Astaire and didn't I play the melodeon for Frankincense and Myrrh.

There he goes – the man what learned me English.

There's a book in everyone. It's not always necessary to publish it and if you can't write it yourself you should let it be drawn out of you by somebody. Afterwards the world will have a fuller understanding of you and many things about you will be explained in a way that is not possible by expiring silently with the whole secret of your life locked up within you and the whole complicated and monumental tale on its way to total decay for bones don't speak and the dust is also silent.

The lazy wretches didn't cut enough turf to make smoke for benediction.

———◆———

You can't teach an old dog new tricks but when his mentors are the mounting years he will learn to share the hearth with the cat.

———◆———

It will be a black day for Dirrabeg if we penalise a man because he has an industrious penis.

———◆———

'Chu Manchu' the dog butcher bar-
ked.

<hr />

The 1930s was the time of the shut
mouth and the closed eye and the
hardened heart. There were two black
clouds covering the pleasant face of
the country. One of them was the
Catholic Church and the other was
the State. They made prisoners of our
minds and bodies and 'twas that
bleak for awhile we were afraid to
take note of the beating of our own
hearts.

One quirk tells me more than all the orthodox aspects put together.

Given the option of attending a funeral or a sex orgy the dyed-in-the-wool Celt will always opt for the funeral.

The secret of sex is not to take it seriously.

I was missing a piece from my complete set of nuisances but now he's just turned up.

Virginity is very like a souvenir, sometimes priceless to its owner but, alas, worth much less in the open market.

<hr>

The doctors in Trallock wouldn't know their balls from their tonsils.

<hr>

You only withdraw what you deposit in the marriage stakes and our romantic deposits are few and far between!

<hr>

People who are ashamed of their addresses should remember that Christ was born in a stable and people who are proud of their addresses should remember it even more.

To destroy a man's character is to relieve him of his most valuable possession and does not the law blame the receiver rather than the disposer of the stolen item. Therefore he who accepts the false account without demur is the real villain.

Please mix me a stomach potion which will stop history repeating itself.

Dare any man come near her and I'll pull off his head like you'd pull a cork off an ink bottle. No. No. No. I'm too lenient. I'll skin the hoor alive and strangle him with his own pelt.

Marriage is a long, difficult confrontation with short outbreaks of peace.

She floated drunkenly into the lounge like a turbulence in the wake of a duck brood on an unruffled pond.

A telegram is a letter of sorts, a stunted one shorn of embellishment, a Beckett of the epistolatory world open to many interpretations, its length dictated by the circumstances of the sender.

The back is the prairie of the anatomy.

There is no lakewater, seawater or rippling cadence as enchanting as the lapping of liquor in a glass held by human hands.

He lived between two brothels for most of his life but was never part of a horizontal pairing.

The pièce de resistance of the visit was the introduction of their two year old prodigy who, at his parents' behest, effed and blinded like a chap twice his age.

I suppose you could say that a chasti-
tute is the opposite of a prostitute.

Patters and pinchers of female poste-
riors make no further advances when
confronted by their victims. The lay-
ing-on of the hand is sufficient in itself to satisfy whatever appetite pre-
cipitated the covert action.

May God preserve us from the awful
stigma of respectability.

The city isn't everything but at least it's got store-bought love and that's better than nothing.

[He] wouldn't give you the dirt under his toe-nails if he thought 'twould do you any good.

Your Kerryman loves words. Snare him with well-chosen ones and craftily-calefacted phrases and he will respond with sempiternal sentences, sonorous and supernatural.

Ireland, as a whole, is a nation chiefly made up of Protestants and Catholics, some of them Christians.

He successfully mingled the safe delights of matrimony with the perilous prurience of infidelity and was ultimately rewarded with a highly favourable mortuary card.

I looked in the mirror this morning but I did not see the face of a president.

Art and life are next-door neighbours but they don't always have a tolerance for each other.

———◆———

Taken in good measure Christmas is the best of all known antidotes for bitterness.

———◆———

Digressions are to my tales what oases are to desert nomads, what the sideline fracas is to the bored onlooker. A story without digressions is like a thoroughfare without side-streets.

———◆———

Better-looking men than me such as vets, inseminators, insurance agents, seed salesmen and warble-fly inspectors seem to enjoy immunity but pull on a postman's uniform and you're a target for every sex-starved damsel in the district.

***

When I was a boy Hell was a terrible place, but in today's Hell a snowball would last a very long time.

***

A house without a liar is like a hearse without a coffin.

He was seduced by a sixty-year old deserted wife when he was fifteen. After that auspicious beginning he never looked back.

Now that progress has deprived the devil of his horns I wonder what modifications they have in mind for God.

The garter was the timberline of morality and the plimsoll line of security. Can the same be said for tights!

As the speech entered its thirtieth minute I applied for and was granted citizenship of the Land of Nod.

A minor bore can be of incalculable assistance in deflecting the attentions of a major bore.

If tables and chairs could talk and windows could give evidence you'd be transported for perjury and you'd never see hide nor light of this country again.

The bohareen* is the last sanctuary of overworked ponies absent without leave, of hare-shy greyhounds and indisposed hedgehogs. It is a true haven for harried souls.

———◆———

The elements are the mentors of Kerrymen. They can patter like rain, roar like thunder, foam like the sea, sting like frost, sigh like the wind and on top of all that you'll never catch them boasting.

———◆———

* *country lane*

I would prefer to write about the living lingo of the greater, hard-necked Atlantical warbler known as the Kerryman who quests individually and in flocks for all forms of diversion and is to be found high and low, winter and summer wherever there is the remotest prospect of sex, booze or commotion.

As I sat I recalled that my own wife's eyes are celestial blue with hints and tints of sapphire and aquamarine.

The double bed is the hatchery of every family plot, the blueprint for designing the features of offspring, the last refuge of the fractured marriage and a great place to hide under if you're a man on the run.

When he dropped dead in Killarney, all that was found in his pockets was a corkscrew.

Before setting out on the skite I made out a cheque to that loveable old rascal known as Self.

A looking-glass does nothing for me but I do have a face which reacts favourably to any kind of a glass with a drink in it.

The most resistant of all materials is to be found in the human skull. It can shut off the brain from incontrovertible truths despite the most consistent bombardment.

Convent dripping will cure all aches.

The majority of those who are presently incarcerated are innocent when compared to those who never close or only partly close doors.

Nothing so affronts the female eye as that cataclysmic calamity of the culinary world, the sunken porter cake.

He is a rare man who can keep down his bias after swallowing it.

A wooden leg is like an adopted child. With all the ups and downs in the world it could be better to you than one of your own in the end.

Bores have their own code, the major feature of which is that one bore never intrudes while another is harassing a victim.

He is such a devout Catholic, he won't be happy until he is crucified.

If only we could package part of love-ly and wonderful occasions and then, on a bleak day, open the package and savour the fragrance of what we once preserved!

We Irish have a distinct flourish. It's like a tail, a Celtic tail. You can't see it but by God it whips us around.

If only the world and its people could wait long enough everybody would be kissed by somebody sometime.

Christmas is like an egg. If you don't take it before its expiry date it will turn rotten.

The chief difference between edible gooseberries and human gooseberries is that the edible are completely covered with hairs whereas the human is only partly covered.

True writing is when you consistently tax yourself till you're frayed almost beyond recovery.

Knife, pale knife, third hand of the coward.

If there's one thing a man is entitled to in this world it's the government he voted for.

A lot of divorces are caused by people who want to resign but have nothing else to resign from.

He wins most at poker who can afford to lose.

I'm ashamed of you Catholic dogs of
Listowel, howling with the Angelus
bell and then soiling the streets.

If you don't find serenity by the sea
on a calm November day you'll prob-
ably never find it.

He's as deep as a well ... as wise as a
book ... as sharp as a scythe ...

I'd swap ten Mondays for one Satur-
day.

In marriage you must remember that
one and one makes one and not two.

There's a cure from the famine times
when the Gaelic sex drive was failing.
Spatter the breastbone with fresh
lakewater when the moon is waxing
and spatter the backbone with the
dews of night when the moon is wan-
ing.

This world is full of people who look
worse than they are.

If she didn't let it out of her mouth, 'twould break out in boils and sores all over her.

He would sooner stick his snout in a plate of mate and cabbage or to rub the back of a fattening pig than whisper a bit of his fondness for her.

You are the bladder of a pig, the snout of a sow; you are the leavings of a hound, the sting of a wasp. You will die roaring.

For every one of us conceived in hay-barns, motor-cars, alley-ways and deserted handball alleys ninety-nine percent of us are born in bed.

Somewhere upstairs I heard the unmistakable sound of wild oats being sown.

You can lie without saying a word; you can lie without opening your lips; you can lie by silence.

You're as hard as nails ... there isn't a belly in the hospitals of Ireland that would throw out a gallstone half as hard as you.

There was more thrown to dogs in our house than was eaten in yours in the round of a year!

You might say he was one of the exceptions which proves the rule that only opposing sexes surrender to each other.

A married couple who don't look worn after a lifetime together have not been doing their job. They remind me of the footballer who comes off the field at the end of the game as fresh as when he first went on.

His feet were like forks of lightning. He would dance on a three-penny bit for you.

They all want the bull but few the calf.

If you could remember that it's only all going through life, that it will even out in the end. What seems awful now will be nothing in the course of time.

Marriage is a great thing until the partner is taken but the conflict may be resumed by taking another.

Women are like the ocean, peaceful and calm one minute and the next violent and raging.

Many's the innocent girl got a suck-in and found herself straddled by a man with no battery in his flash lamp ... men will boast and women foolish enough to believe will be disappointed and deceived.

———◆———

A man who has not been made to eat humble pie has had a diet without roughage. I would look upon the eating of humble pie as a major developing factor in the human character.

———◆———

I love whiskey. I love the gurgle of it in the snout of the bottle and I love the rich plop when it falls into a glass. I love the way it babbles and bubbles when a bottle is shaken. As for the taste of it I find it goes beyond words. That first drop of it hits the walls of the chest with a ferocious rattle but after that it lights up the interior and there is a wonderful lunacy in the head.

———◆———

Play the fool to be thought a fool and you'll get away with murder.

———◆———

Remember that every time you think about, talk to, kiss or caress a woman your heart beats at several times the normal speed. Now the heart has only so many beats and when these are exhausted there is that awful struggle for breath, that ultimate cry of anguish and despair and finally that last terrible gasp ... if by merely thinking about women the heart beats faster imagine the speed if a man makes total love to a woman ...

———◆———

Life is the grimmest loan of all. The interest is too high at the end.

The unattached women of today burn up vodka and gin as if they had jet engines inside. If it made them drunk itself, but what happens is that they become more crafty.

When did we ever see a man on his knees scrubbing the kitchen floor? When I see it I'll eat the scrubbing brush.

Pubs are filled with men who need recognition for unrecognised talents.

Yesterday they promised bright spells and if you had binoculars you would not find the blue of a child's eye in the sky.

Greatness is no guarantee of happiness.

There was no grandeur about him. He always blew his nose into his palm and rubbed it to the seat of his trousers and he never used anything but his coat sleeve to clean his face.

God help him he's cursed with a terrible tooth for porter.

There is no gander as vulgar, there's no magpie as raucous and there's no badger as grey or mottled and to think she calls herself a Christian.

He has become a spent force, he is a smolt who will never again return to the clear and sparkling waters of the upriver reeds.

Our friend the unlicensed bull who only wants to play the role of lover and father is denied these basic rights and consigned to a life of ineffectuality because of the whimsical preferences which presently prevail in the Department of Agriculture.

It is also a known fact that when men of no property aspire to property they quickly shed their socialistic tendencies.

Bite me, kick me, curse me but touch my drinking hand at your peril.

To be rejected by a female is merely to be seasoned for a second assault upon the citadel of romance.

***

You should never set traps unless you are prepared to fall into one some time.

***

He dug her garden, thinned her lettuce, rebuilt her coal-shed, lopped her branches but failed to make the slightest impression on her chastity.

There is no such entity as a conventional Kerryman. If you try to analyse him he changes his pace in order to generate confusion. He will not be pinned down and you have as much chance of getting a straight answer out of him as you would a goose egg out of an Arctic tern.

———◦◦◦———

Idleness, we are told, makes a mockery of morals. Idleness too, it might be said, is the chief nourishment of lust.

———◦◦◦———

You may make hay while the sun shines and you may stook turf when the wind blows but as sure as there's mate on the shin of a wren there's more to be made working the head at the shady side of a ditch on a wet day.

For all that may be said in favour of electric blankets and hot-water bottles, there is nothing to equal the blissful heat of a partner's body after coming in from the cold of a winter's night.

He's fit for nothing only mischief –
the same as a bull in August.

* * *

They say in Kerry that being born in
Kerry is the greatest gift that God can
bestow on any man, that when you
belong to Kerry you know you have a
head start on the other fellow.

* * *

It is not by contradicting liars that we
make them tell the truth but rather by
exaggerating in the same vein.

* * *

Some men are wild for drink, some for money and more for travel but there's others and sex comes as natural to them as it does to the puck or the pony stallion.

Men who leave fortunes behind when they pass on are rarely remembered for long. When the resources they carefully husbanded through life are exhausted by the profligate heirs so does the memory of the benefactor also expire.

The golf club tease modestly bent her head every time she crossed her long bare legs.

If you want to be remembered by your relations the best thing to do is to leave a few modest debts behind you. You won't be remembered affectionately but you will be remembered.

A young wan should make the most of her dreams before her belly rises.

Be liberal with your relatives. Give them away cheerfully.

Jealousy is the worst disease of all and there's no medicine for it.

I know nothing about him except that his father was cashiered out of the Black and Tans.

[He has] the cuteness of a pet fox and the long distance eye of a starving gannet.

She had long legs which transmitted bustle and life to the bouncing buttocks overhead.

***

He dragged his feet after him as though they were somebody else's.

***

Though the bit was in her mouth ... she was never rightly broke.

***

The bigger the tree the smaller the apple, the smaller the bush the bigger the berry.

I have only one life and the Catechism don't say nothing about courting or coupling in the hereafter.

He was the most marvellous liar I ever heard and while he talked about me I was so carried away that I thought I was listening to the life story of a saint.

You have no way of knowing the meaning of grief until it lifts the latch on your own door.

Reeling drunkenly home from the broad strands of Ballybunion with the salty tang of a mermaid's kisses pricking his lips.

———◆———

His vocal cords are that frayed from whiskey he couldn't raise his voice these days if it was to save his life. The man is a walking brewery. You must be colour blind if you haven't noticed his nose. 'Tis like the end of a purple black pudding ...

———◆———

Judge a man by his telegrams if you want his essence.

He is often obliged to harness the chariot of the law to the horses of humanity.

We have muddied the ground like a bull at the gate of a heifer field.

If there were not a seamy side to life there would be no necessity for custodians of the peace.

He drinks like a fish but he doesn't splash.

[She] is one of those strong-willed women who will never latch onto a made man. They prefer to start with their own raw material, no matter how rugged or crude and to mould what they want out of that. The husbands have no say whatsoever in the outcome ...

The law is like a woman's knickers, full of dynamite and elastic and best left to those who have the legal right and qualifications to handle it properly.

I could a tale unfold ... about this village ... that would make the *News of the World* read like a Communion tract ...

A marriage without a row is like apple pie without cloves.

A cut-jack is a stallion ass or in electrical terms an ass whose light bulb has been taken from its socket, or, if you like, a donkey with a diminished under-carriage.

There is no cowardice worse than the cowardice of parents who will not face up to the facts, who refuse to recognise that rearing children to be useful members of society is a full-time, complicated, sensitive vocation without parallel in the whole range of serious callings.

The seeds of one argument should not be saved to foster another.

As apprehensive as a donkey in illicit postures.

He had the longest reach I ever saw in a human being if there was anything to be grabbed that cost nothing.

The great stag that is human dignity is humbled and dragged down by the hounds of self-indulgence.

If you weigh the character of the detractor against that of his victim you'll find that the latter always comes out on top.

He sired them on the tops of mountains and the depths of valleys, up against hall doors and half-doors, against hawthorn hedges, turf-ricks and oat-stacks, in rain or shine, on dry ground or puddle, in the backs of motor-cars and in the fronts of motor-cars, upstairs and downstairs, in hay sheds and turf sheds, byres and barns, in nooks and crannies and all over the place till he transported himself through necessity across the wide Atlantic.

<hr/>

In togs she had a large white belly like a harvest frog.

While these domineering task-masters were inclined to put up with such crimes as murder, rape and incest with good-natured tolerance they could not and would not suffer the sin of idleness around the farm.

Grey hairs are the harbingers of tolerance and maturity.

The best thrill of all they say is to rub the head of a baldy man. You can feel his brains underneath and tell what he might be thinking.

Give me a lie anytime before a wilful silence, a silence that watches coldly and callously while evil smothers good.

***

In its own time and in its own place and in conditions blessed by love the kiss will melt the icicles of frigidity and replace the pinched cheek with the amorous suffusion.

***

He has the same chance as a three-legged hare at a coursing meeting.

***

The most daring of males will invent the most outrageous lies to save themselves, to justify an injustice, to convince themselves that wrong is right and to seduce and subsequently ravish innocent females.

She spread herself all over the company like a hen preparing to hatch.

There was a body to her chuckle like boiling tar.

An affair is a mere sneeze which gathers slowly and disperses quickly.

I might have been a chap of infinite morality, a veritable paragon had I not been let down by the most contumacious pudenda.

What a wonderful fellow I would be but for this baggage of reproduction which demoralises my every thought and deed.

It was about as philosophical an inanity as the nocturnal braying of a wandering jackass.

———◆———

I fantasise about whiskey the way other men fantasise about women.

———◆———

I am not a drunkard. I was born into this world with a true appreciation of whiskey.

———◆———

All this talking has left my mouth as dry as the inside of a crypt.